W9-CHR-831

MUSTARD

CHARLOTTE GRAEBER

MUSTARD

Illustrated by Donna Diamond

Macmillan Publishing Co., Inc.

New York

Macmillan Publishing Co., Inc.
866 Third Avenue, New York, N.Y. 10022
Collier Macmillan Canada, Inc.
Printed in the United States of America

10 9 8 7 6 5 4 3 2 1

LIBRARY OF CONGRESS CATALOGING IN PUBLICATION DATA
Graeber, Charlotte Towner.   Mustard.
SUMMARY: Eight-year-old Alex and his family try to come
to terms with the old age and death of their beloved cat.
[1. Cats—Fiction. 2. Pets—Fiction. 3. Death—Fiction]
I. Diamond, Donna, ill.   II. Title.
PZ7.G75153Mu [Fic] 81-20764 ISBN 0-02-736690-1 AACR2

*In memory of my husband, Vance,
and our own cat, Juju*

—C. G.

For Elaine and Joel, with love

—D. D.

CHAPTER ONE

"Ow!" Annie cried. "Mustard scratched me!"

Alex looked at his little sister's arm. Two red scratches marked her wrist. Nearby, the cat, Mustard, was lying under the table. His large yellow eyes were narrowed into slits. And his puffy orange-yellow tail swished in anger.

"What were you doing to him?" Alex asked. He saw Annie's doll bonnet lying on the floor. "Playing dress up again?"

"I want Mustard to wear a blue bonnet." Annie sniffed loudly.

Just then Mom came into the living room.

"Mustard hurt me, Mom," Annie complained.

"She was trying to dress him up again," Alex said. He did not blame Mustard for scratching Annie. What cat liked to be dressed up like a baby?

Mom examined the scratches. "I'll bet that hurts," she said. "We'll put something on them to make them feel better."

Annie nodded. Then she stomped over to where Mustard was lying. She shook her fist at the cat. "Bad Mustard!" she announced. "Bad cat!"

But Mustard only swished his tail and turned the other way.

"You shouldn't bother Mustard all the time," Mom said. She got an antiseptic spray and a bandage out of the closet. "Sometimes Mustard wants to be left alone."

Alex watched Mom dab Annie's scratches. He knew the scratches hurt. Mustard had scratched him lots of times. But he never cried about it.

"Mustard is mean," Annie said. "He won't play with me."

Mom unwrapped the bandage strip and placed it on Annie's wrist. "Mustard is just getting old," she said. ·

Alex frowned. Mustard was not *that* old. He just did not like to be teased. "Mustard is not old," Alex said.

Mom looked thoughtful. "Mustard is old in cat years, Alex," she said. "Why, he must be older than Grandpa Covey. Older, even, than Mr. Sommers."

Alex felt a lump fill his stomach. Grandpa Covey didn't seem old. He jogged every day and played tennis with Dad on weekends. But Mr. Sommers who lived across the street? He was really old. He had white hair and walked with a shuffle. He couldn't see very well even with his glasses on. And just last Christmas Mr. Sommers had a heart attack. The paramedics had rushed him to the hospital in the middle of the night.

Alex faced Mom with his fists clenched. "Mustard is not old," he insisted. "He runs and plays all the time." He turned to Annie. "You shouldn't be teasing him all the time. No cat wants a bonnet on his head!" He reached under the table and scooped Mustard into his arms. "You are only as old as you feel," he said firmly. "That's what Grandpa Covey said when he beat Dad at tennis."

He marched out of the room to the enclosed porch. Mus-

3

tard purred deeply as Alex placed him on the rug. Then he batted wildly at a rubber ball Annie had left on the floor.

All at once Mustard sat up with his ears twitching. In one leap he was on the table by the porch windows.

Alex looked out. Jeff Reed was coming down the street with his papers. And his big black and white dog, Barney, was right behind him. Alex wished Jeff would leave his dog at home. He always upset Mustard.

Mustard snarled deep in his throat. His tail thumped on the tabletop. Barney raced across the yard toward the house. He leaped up at the windows, barking wildly.

"Stop that!" Alex hollered. "Go away!"

Jeff tossed the newspaper onto the steps, then pedaled away. Barney raced down the block after him. But Mustard stayed by the windows. His yellow eyes watched the dog until he was out of sight.

At supper Annie showed Dad her scratches. "Mustard did it," she said. "He is getting old."

Alex stopped eating. "It was her fault, Dad," he said. "She was trying to tie a bonnet on his head."

Dad laughed. "I don't think I'd like a bonnet on *my* head."

Just then Mustard meowed under the table. He brushed against Alex's ankles.

"He is not too old to beg for food," Dad said. He cut a small piece of meat and fed it to Mustard.

Alex made a face at Annie.

And Annie made a face back.

"Stop it, you two," Dad said. Then he turned to Mom. "How old is Mustard, anyway? He must be close to twelve."

"Mustard is fourteen," Mom said. "Remember? You gave him to me that first Easter."

Dad nodded.

"I thought it was a baby rabbit at first." Mom grinned across the table at Dad.

Alex had heard the story about Mustard lots of times. Dad had wanted a special Easter gift for Mom. He picked out the kitten at the animal shelter.

"And Mom named him Mustard," Annie said.

"Mustard because of his orange-yellow color," Mom said.

"And because Dad likes mustard," Alex added. Dad put mustard on almost everything he ate. Even scrambled eggs.

Dad sighed. "It seems like only yesterday."

Suddenly Mustard meowed and leaped onto Dad's lap.

"Oh, no you don't," Dad said. He picked Mustard up and set him firmly on the floor.

"Speaking of Mustard," Mom said, "I think it's time for his yearly checkup."

"Mustard hates the animal doctor," Alex said.

"It is for his own good," Mom said. "I think I'll take him tomorrow, before I put it off."

Mustard crept back under the table. It seemed he knew what Mom was talking about.

"Can I go with you?" Alex asked. "After school?"

"Well," said Mom. "I have to take Annie to ballet class. I guess we could take Mustard to the veterinarian in the same trip."

Alex leaned down from his chair. "Don't worry, Mustard," he said. "I won't let the doctor hurt you."

Dad laughed. "The question is—will Mustard hurt the veterinarian?"

CHAPTER TWO

The next afternoon Alex and Mom dropped Annie at her ballet school. Then they took Mustard to the animal clinic at the edge of town. The waiting room was empty except for a man paying his bill. Mom stepped to the counter. Alex sat down on a red chair. He held Mustard on a blanket on his lap.

Mustard tried to burrow under the blanket.

"Don't worry, Mustard," Alex whispered. "No one is going to hurt you."

Mustard meowed and tucked his head under Alex's arm.

At the counter, Mom gave Mustard's name and address. A woman took a card out of a large file cabinet.

"It will be a few minutes," she said.

Soon the veterinarian opened the door to the examination rooms. His name was Dr. Griffith. He wore a green doctor's coat and a tie with dog pictures on it.

"I'm ready for Mustard," he said.

Mustard yowled and leaped off Alex's lap.

"I don't think Mustard is ready for you," Mom laughed.

Alex picked Mustard up. "Can I bring Mustard in?" he asked.

Dr. Griffith glanced at Mom. And Mom shrugged.

"O.K.," said Dr. Griffith. He led the way to a small room with a high table, a white cabinet and one window. It looked very clean. It smelled clean, too.

Dr. Griffith took Mustard from Alex and placed him on the table. "Let's have a look at you, old boy," he said.

Alex frowned. Why did everyone call Mustard old?

Mustard tried to scoot off the table. But Mom caught him and held him tight. "No one is going to hurt you, Mustard," she said softly. Mustard lay down and glared up at Dr. Griffith.

Without speaking, Dr. Griffith opened Mustard's mouth. He poked inside with a flat wooden stick. "His teeth are in good shape," he said. Next he took a small flashlight from the cabinet. He turned it on and shone the light into each of Mustard's ears. "His ears seem fine."

Mustard squirmed and growled low in his throat. Mom grabbed his front paws to keep him from scratching. Dr. Griffith ignored Mustard's growls. Instead he flashed the light into Mustard's yellow eyes.

"There is some cloudiness in the left eye," he said.

Alex held his breath. He didn't want Mustard to have trouble seeing.

Dr. Griffith moved the light back and forth. And Mustard turned his eyes to follow it.

"It doesn't seem to affect his vision," Dr. Griffith said at last.

Then Dr. Griffith examined Mustard's stomach, throat and hindquarters. He placed one hand on Mustard's chest and held it there a long time.

"Mustard's breathing is irregular," he said finally. He turned to the cabinet for a stethoscope. "This is a doctor's tool for listening to the lungs and heart," he explained to Alex.

Alex nodded. He knew that already. He stepped closer to the table. He felt afraid.

Dr. Griffith placed one end of the stethoscope on Mustard's chest. He placed two tubes at the other end in his ears. Then he leaned down to listen.

Mustard lay very still. And Alex held his breath. His own heart was beating like an Indian drum.

At last Dr. Griffith stood up. "Mustard is in good shape for an old cat," he began. He glanced at Alex. "But his heart is not as strong as it used to be."

Alex felt his throat tighten. Mom reached down to squeeze his hand.

"Is it very serious?" she asked.

Dr. Griffith put the stethoscope away. "Mustard is an old-timer for a cat. It is natural for him to slow down."

Alex thought about Mr. Sommers shuffling around his backyard. Would Mustard slow down like that?

Dr. Griffith stepped to the cabinet. "Now for Mustard's yearly shot," he said.

Before Alex knew it, Dr. Griffith had given Mustard the shot. Then he took a green bottle from the cabinet. "I want you to give Mustard some vitamins," he said. "As for his heart . . ." He handed the bottle to Mom. "Mustard should take things easy. No stress and no excitement."

Alex nodded. Mom nodded, too, and placed Mustard in Alex's arms.

"Don't worry, Dr. Griffith," Alex said. "I'll take good care of Mustard."

Mom and Alex followed Dr. Griffith back to the waiting room. Mustard rubbed his head against Alex's chin. His loud purr rumbled in Alex's ears.

CHAPTER THREE

At home Mom told Annie and Dad what Dr. Griffith had said. "Mustard's heart is not as strong as it could be," she said.

"He is not supposed to have any stress," Alex added.

"What's stress?" Annie asked.

"Stress is putting a doll bonnet on Mustard's head when he doesn't like it," Dad explained.

Mustard meowed at Mom's feet. He turned in a full circle and held one paw up.

"Stress is not getting fed when he's hungry," Mom said.

She opened a can of Mustard's food. Mustard sat by his red bowl waiting.

"This is a good time to start his vitamins," Mom said. She got the bottle from her purse. She unscrewed the cap with the built-in dropper.

Alex watched Mom fill the dropper and mix the vitamins into Mustard's food. Mom set the bowl in front of Mustard.

Mustard meowed as he lowered his head to the food. Then he looked up at Mom. He didn't like the vitamins in his food. He sniffed the bowl and walked away.

"You can't fool a smart cat like Mustard," Dad said.

"Eat your food, Mustard," Annie said. "It's good for you."

Alex picked Mustard up and set him in front of his bowl again. But it was no use. Mustard would not eat the food. He arched his back and stalked away.

"Oh, no you don't, Mr. Mustard Cat," Mom said. She scooped Mustard up and set him on her lap. She refilled the dropper with vitamins. Then she pried Mustard's mouth open with one hand.

Mustard growled, and his tail swished. But Mom held on.

"Don't hurt him!" Annie cried. "He doesn't like vitamins!"

But Mom leaned forward and placed the dropper by Mustard's mouth.

All at once Mustard butted Mom's hand away. He jumped off her lap and landed on the kitchen table. Mom squirted the vitamins on the floor.

"There has to be an easier way," Mom said. She mopped up the floor with a rag.

"I have an idea," Dad said. He grabbed an old towel out of the closet. "We'll wrap Mustard up so he can't get away."

First Dad wrapped the towel around Mustard's neck and shoulders. Then he folded it over his body and feet. Soon only Mustard's head poked out. He looked very angry.

But Dad's idea worked. Mom gave Mustard the vitamins with no trouble. When she was done, Dad unwrapped the towel. Mustard jumped from the table to the floor. He sat with his tail swishing.

"You have to stop getting upset, Mustard," Alex told him. "It isn't good for you."

"It isn't good for Mustard to be hungry," Mom said. She cleaned out his bowl. She refilled it with fresh food and set it on the floor.

Mustard sniffed the food. Then he looked up at Dad.

"There are no vitamins in your food," Dad said.

Mustard sniffed the food again. Slowly he lowered his head and began eating. When he was done he crossed the kitchen and lay down in front of the stove. He began to wash his whiskers with one paw.

The next day Alex stayed after school. When he got home, Jeff Reed was coming down the block with Barney.

Alex ran into the house. In the kitchen, Mustard was sitting on the window sill. His ears were flattened against his head, and his tail was swishing.

Alex tried to grab Mustard. But Mustard hissed and lashed at the glass with both paws.

On the steps outside, Annie shook her fists at Barney. "Go away, bad dog!" she yelled.

But Barney bounded across the lawn and sprang up snarling at Mustard.

At last Alex lifted Mustard off the window sill. Mustard hissed and scratched. But Alex carried him through the house to his room. He could feel Mustard's heart thumping against his chest. Was it beating too fast?

"You have to stop fighting with Barney," Alex said. He closed the door and set Mustard on the bed.

Mustard blinked at Alex. Then he turned in a circle and lay down. Alex watched Mustard's chest rise and fall with each breath.

"I'll protect you," Alex said. "I won't let Barney get you."

Mustard curled his body into a letter *C* and closed his eyes. He began to purr. The purring sounded like a motorboat engine. It was the loudest purr in the world.

CHAPTER FOUR

Mom gave Mustard one dropper full of vitamins every day. Mustard got used to being held in the old towel. He stopped growling and trying to jump away.

Each day, Alex kept Mustard in his room until Jeff and Barney went by. Annie promised not to tease Mustard or dress him in doll clothes.

In a few weeks the leaf buds on the trees began to open. Mom's tulips bloomed red and yellow and white.

Everyone was busy. Alex washed and polished his bicycle. Dad spent Saturdays turning over the garden with a spade.

Alex stopped worrying about Mustard's heart. He stopped

watching Mustard breathe. Mustard played with his catnip mouse. And he chased his own tail like always. There was nothing wrong with Mustard.

Instead, Alex thought about his treehouse. As soon as it turned warm, he would start to build it. Dad gave him the old wood in the garage. He gave him his hammer to use and a box of nails.

One day the sun was warmer than usual. The birds hopped among the branches of the trees. Alex hurried home from school to start building. He would have a treehouse in the big maple by Easter time.

In his room Alex changed into his old clothes.

"Be careful," Mom said. "Don't climb too high."

Alex did not see Mustard waiting at the back door. He did not think about Mustard wanting to get outside. When he opened the door, Mustard scooted out.

"Mustard! Come back here!" Alex shouted. He chased the cat around the side of the house. But Mustard had disappeared. Alex could not see him anywhere.

"Mom!" Alex called. "Mustard got out! He is hiding somewhere!"

Annie hurried outside. But Mom opened an upstairs window. "I don't think it will hurt Mustard to get some fresh air," she said. "He has been cooped up all winter."

Alex crouched down to look under the bushes. There sat Mustard watching a black beetle crawl along the ground. Mom was right. Mustard loved to be outside. He would come back when he was hungry.

Alex dragged a stack of old boards across the backyard. He put the nails in one pocket. He stuck the hammer in another. Then he climbed to the first branch of the maple tree.

Annie stood on the ground watching.

"Hand me one of the boards," Alex called down.

He nailed the first board across the tree trunk. Then he climbed higher. Soon he had three board steps nailed to the tree.

Just then he heard the bang of the newspaper against the front door. Barney came tearing around the house.

"Mom! Mom!" Alex yelled. He raced to the bushes where Mustard sat.

But Barney got there ahead of Alex. Mustard came out of the bushes with his feet flying. He hissed and yowled and

struck out at the big dog. Barney struck back with his teeth bared in a snarl.

"Barney!" Jeff Reed yelled. He ran into the yard and tried to grab Barney's collar.

But the big dog leaped away. He chased Mustard around the house and under the front porch.

"He's got my cat cornered!" Alex hollered. "Get him out of here!"

Finally, Jeff grabbed Barney's collar and pulled him away from the porch. The dog's nose was bleeding. "Your cat scratched Barney's nose," he said.

Annie lay on her stomach looking under the porch. "Mustard," she pleaded. "Come out."

Mom raced out of the house. "What happened?" She reached under the porch and pulled Mustard out. He lay on one side breathing very fast. His yellow eyes were wide and glazed with fear.

"Mom! Mustard is hurt!" Alex cried.

Mom carried Mustard into the house. She laid him on the porch rug. "Annie, get a blanket!" she said. "Alex, get a bowl of water!"

Alex ran to the kitchen. He should have been paying attention. He should have remembered Barney would be following Jeff when he delivered the evening paper.

Mustard wanted to drink the water. But he couldn't lift his head.

"What's wrong with him, Mom?" Alex asked.

"I think he's in shock," Mom said. She covered him with the blanket Annie held.

Mom put on her coat and picked up her purse. Then she lifted Mustard into her arms. "Hurry up! We've got to get Mustard to the vet," she said. "He'll know what to do."

Alex and Annie hurried down the front walk after Mom. At the car they got in back together.

Mom lay Mustard on the front seat beside her. Then she started the car and pulled away from the curb.

"Is Mustard going to die?" Annie asked. Tears filled her eyes and rolled down her cheeks.

Alex shook his head. He didn't know how to answer.

CHAPTER FIVE

Dr. Griffith said Mustard had had a heart attack. The chase with Barney brought it on. At the clinic he gave Mustard a shot of special medicine for his heart. And he gave Mom a bottle of medicine to take home. The medicine was bright pink. Mom was supposed to give it to Mustard twice a day.

Mom settled Mustard on his favorite chair in the living room.

"Is he going to die?" Annie asked.

Alex glared at his sister. "Is he going to be all right, Mom?" he asked.

Mom shook her head. "It is too soon to tell. Dr. Griffith said he will know better in a few days."

Alex felt his throat catch. And hot tears pushed at his eyelids.

Annie began to cry. Dad lifted her onto his lap. "Mustard is an old cat," he said. "We'll do all we can for him."

Alex thought about Mr. Sommers. Mr. Sommers had had a heart attack. He was still alive. "People get better from heart attacks," Alex said. "Mustard will, too."

In his room Alex made a special bed for Mustard. He put his softest pillow on the floor next to the radiator. Mom said it would be a warm, quiet place.

Annie put her teddy bear next to the pillow. "To keep Mustard company," she said.

After supper Alex placed Mustard on his special bed. Then he sat down on the floor. He petted Mustard's soft fur gently. "I'll be right here. I'll be right here if you need me," he said.

Mustard pushed his head against Alex's knee. Then he went to sleep.

At bedtime Dad came in to tell Alex good night. He leaned

down to rub Mustard's ears. "Good old Mustard. Good old fellow," he said softly. Then he sat down on Alex's bed. "Alex," he began, "sometimes people do not get better from heart attacks."

Alex pushed his feet deep into the cool sheets. "Sometimes they do, Dad," he said. "Like Mr. Sommers."

Dad sighed. "Sometimes they do." He pulled the blanket over Alex's shoulders. "But sometimes a heart just stops . . ." Dad paused. "And life is over."

Alex turned away from Dad. He scrunched his face into the pillow. He did not want to think about life ending. Not for Mustard.

"Good night, Alex," Dad said. "I wish I could tell you Mustard will be O.K. But we can only hope."

When Dad left, Alex climbed back out of bed. He hurried to the pillow where Mustard lay. He crouched down and kissed the top of Mustard's head. "Get better, Mustard," he said. "I don't want you to die."

Mustard's loud purr rippled against Alex's cheek. And Alex went back to bed.

It was dark when Alex woke up. He heard a bumping sound. Then he heard Mustard cry out. Alex turned on the light. Mustard was not on the pillow. He was not at the foot of the bed where he sometimes slept. Alex could not see Mustard anywhere. But he heard him. The awful cry sounded again.

"Dad!" Alex yelled. "Something is wrong with Mustard. But I can't find him!"

Both Dad and Mom rushed into Alex's room. Then Dad found Mustard. He was in the closet pacing from one corner to the other. He was bumping into the walls.

"Dad! What's wrong with him?" Alex sobbed.

Mustard yowled again. Dad carried him out of the closet. When Dad set him down, Mustard began moving in circles. His yellow eyes were wide and blank. When he tried to walk, he wobbled sideways.

"Mustard can't see! He can't walk straight!" Alex cried. "Do something, Dad!"

Mom began to cry.

Dad picked up Mustard and cradled him in his arms. "Go

on back to bed, Alex," he said softly. "We'll take Mustard to our room." Dad started for the door. He turned. "We'll watch him for you."

"I'll get his medicine," Mom said. She ran ahead of Dad to the kitchen.

Alex crawled into bed and turned off the light. But he couldn't go to sleep. He kept hearing Mustard's loud cry. He wanted to ask Dad if Mustard was dying. But he was afraid.

CHAPTER SIX

When Alex woke up, the sun was shining. It was time to get ready for school. Then Alex remembered. Last night Mustard couldn't see. Last night he stumbled in the closet.

Alex jumped out of bed and ran to the kitchen. Dad sat near the window holding Mustard on his lap.

"He doesn't want to eat. Or drink," Dad said.

Mom sat at the kitchen table. Her eyes were red. She was holding the bottle of Mustard's medicine. "He won't swallow his medicine," she said.

Alex walked to Dad's chair. "You have to eat, Mustard," he said. "You have to take your medicine."

Mustard tried to get up, but he could not lift his head. He fell back on Dad's lap. All at once he cried out. And the sound was terrible.

"Dad! Do something!" Alex pleaded.

Mom stood up quickly. "Get ready for school, Alex," she said.

Alex put his hand on Mustard's head. "I don't want to go to school. I want to stay with Mustard."

Dad shook his head. "I'm taking Mustard to the vet this morning," he said. "I want you to go to school."

For a moment Alex stood petting Mustard. "Can Dr. Griffith make Mustard better, Dad? Can he?"

"I don't think Mustard is going to get better," Dad said.

Mom put her elbows on the table. She covered her face with her hands. "All Dr. Griffith can do now is stop Mustard's pain."

Alex looked from Mom to Dad. Dad placed a hand on Alex's shoulder.

"Veterinarians can stop an animal's suffering," he explained. "Dr. Griffith can give Mustard something . . . something to help him die in peace."

Alex stood very still. The room was very quiet. All at once Mustard's legs thrashed wildly. He opened his mouth and cried out again.

Alex ran out of the kitchen. He did not want to see Mustard suffering. He did not want to hear him cry with pain. In his room he stood by the window. He saw Dad when he walked to the car with Mustard in his arms.

On the way to school Jeff Reed came up to Alex. "How's your cat?" he asked. "Old Barney really gave him a chase yesterday."

Alex glared at Jeff. "Old Barney gave Mustard a heart attack. My Dad took him to the vet this morning."

Jeff shuffled his feet and cleared his throat. "Gee, I'm sorry. Is he going to be all right?"

Alex looked down at his shoes. "I don't know," he said. "I don't think so."

Jeff shrugged. And Alex walked away.

Alex could not do his schoolwork. Did Dr. Griffith give

Mustard something to stop his heart? Was Mustard dead already?

At three-thirty Alex ran straight home. Dad's car was in the driveway. Alex raced into the kitchen where he had last seen Mustard. But no one was there. He looked into the backyard.

Dad was standing by the lilac bushes. He was leaning on a shovel. At his feet lay a small cardboard box. Alex's heart pounded against his ribs. His throat ached. He knew what Dad was doing! He knew what was inside the box! He and Annie had buried a dead bird last fall. They had buried a dead chipmunk, too.

"Dad! Dad!" Alex called as he ran outside.

Dad looked up. He caught Alex in his arms and held him tight. "I've been waiting for you," he said.

"Mustard is dead, isn't he?" Alex cried. He tried not to look at the box.

Dad nodded. "There was nothing Dr. Griffith could do."

Alex looked at the box. He had to see for himself. "Can I see him, Dad? Can I look at Mustard now?"

Dad straightened up. For a moment he didn't move. Then

he leaned down and opened the box. He pulled back one end of Annie's old doll blanket.

Alex stared down at Mustard. He did not look dead. He looked asleep. Alex crouched down beside the box. He reached out and touched Mustard's orange head. But Mustard did not move. His body was not warm. Mustard was dead.

"Good old Mustard," Alex sobbed. His tears fell onto Mustard's fur and disappeared.

Dad pulled the blanket back over Mustard's body. He closed the box and placed it in the hole. Then he covered the box with dirt.

Alex watched until the hole was filled. Then he ran into the house. Mom and Annie were standing watching from the window. He rushed past them to his room. The pillow was still on the floor. It still held the shape of Mustard's body.

Alex sat down and laid his head on the pillow. A tuft of orange fur tickled his nose.

CHAPTER SEVEN

The next day Mom gathered Mustard's things. She washed his red food dish and his yellow water bowl. She got his favorite yarn ball from under the sofa. Finally she dug Mustard's cat basket out of the closet.

"Would you like to keep Mustard's collar?" she asked Alex.

Alex picked up the blue collar. It had a shiny gold buckle and a round tag. The tag said: MY NAME IS MUSTARD. I LIVE AT 78 N. GROVE AVE. It had their telephone number on it. Alex thought he would put the collar on his bicycle. He would buckle it around the handlebars so he would see it every day.

"I want to keep Mustard's catnip mouse," Annie said. She picked up the half-chewed toy.

"We will give the rest to the animal shelter," Mom said. She placed everything inside Mustard's basket.

"Where's the shelter?" Annie asked. "Can I go?"

"The shelter is where I first saw Mustard," Dad said. "It is a place for animals that need homes."

"You have a ballet lesson this morning," Mom said to Annie.

"Would you like to go with me, Alex?" Dad asked.

Alex nodded. "Yes, I want to go."

The animal shelter was a one-story building on a sloping hill. All around were fields and trees. Dad drove to the end of the long drive and parked. He waited for Alex to get out of the car. Then he lifted out the basket of Mustard's things. Together they walked to the red-brick building.

Inside, a woman sat at a low counter. One man was just leaving with a puppy in his arms. A woman and a laughing little girl hurried out with him.

Dad put the basket on the counter and sat down on a stool. The woman looked up.

"Can I help you?" she asked.

"I want to give some things to the shelter," Dad said. "Our cat died yesterday."

"Oh, I'm sorry," the woman said. She slid the basket across the counter. Then she looked down at Alex. "I'm sorry you lost your pet."

Alex nodded and looked away.

Dad took out his checkbook. "I'd like to make a donation, too," he said. "I got Mustard here when he was just a kitten." Dad paused and cleared his throat. "Fourteen years ago. At Easter time."

The woman nodded as Dad took out his pen.

"Mustard was a good cat," Dad said, wiping his eyes.

Alex stepped close to Dad. "Mustard had the best purr in the whole world," he said to the woman.

The woman blinked her eyes, too. "Maybe you would like to get another cat," she said. "We have some darling kittens right now."

Dad turned to Alex. "Another cat? Right now?"

Alex shook his head. He did not want another cat. He only wanted Mustard back again. He wanted his old cat.

"No," Dad said to the woman. "We don't want another cat. Not now." He finished writing the check. "Maybe later on." He stood up and handed the check to the woman. Then he took Alex's hand and started toward the door.

Alex could hear dogs barking beyond the room. He saw a sign that said: NO CHILDREN UNDER FIVE.

At the doorway Dad stopped and turned. The woman was still watching them.

"Maybe next spring," Dad said to her. "Maybe *next* Easter time we'll be back for another cat."

Alex followed Dad outside. High in an oak tree a large crow flapped its black wings and crowed. From somewhere nearby another crow answered. Alex took a deep breath of fresh air. Maybe in another year he *would* want another cat. But now he only had room for remembering Mustard.